Room Enough for Daisy

DEBBY
WALDMAN
and
RITA
FEUTL

illustrations by
CINDY REVELL

ORCA BOOK PUBLISHERS

Library and Archives Canada Cataloguing in Publication

Waldman, Debby
Room enough for Daisy / by Debby Waldman and
Rita Feutl ; illustrated by Cindy Revell.

Issued also in electronic format.
ISBN 978-1-55469-255-2

I. Feutl, Rita, 1959- II. Revell, Cindy, 1961- III. Title.
PS8645.A457R66 2011   jc813'.6   C2011-903471-9

First published in the United States, 2011
Library of Congress Control Number: 2011929243

Summary: Daisy thinks her room is too small to fit all the birthday presents she plans to receive, but she realizes she already has everything she needs to be happy and donates many of her belongings to a Mitzvah Day rummage sale.

Orca Book Publishers is dedicated to preserving the environment and has printed this book on paper certified by the Forest Stewardship Council®.

Orca Book Publishers gratefully acknowledges the support for its publishing programs provided by the following agencies: the Government of Canada through the Canada Book Fund and the Canada Council for the Arts, and the Province of British Columbia through the BC Arts Council and the Book Publishing Tax Credit.

Cover and interior artwork created digitally using Corel Painter.

Cover artwork by Cindy Revell
Design by Teresa Bubela

ORCA BOOK PUBLISHERS
PO Box 5626, STN. B
Victoria, BC Canada
V8R 6S4

ORCA BOOK PUBLISHERS
PO Box 468
Custer, WA USA
98240-0468

www.orcabook.com
Printed and bound in Canada.

14 13 12 11 • 4 3 2 1

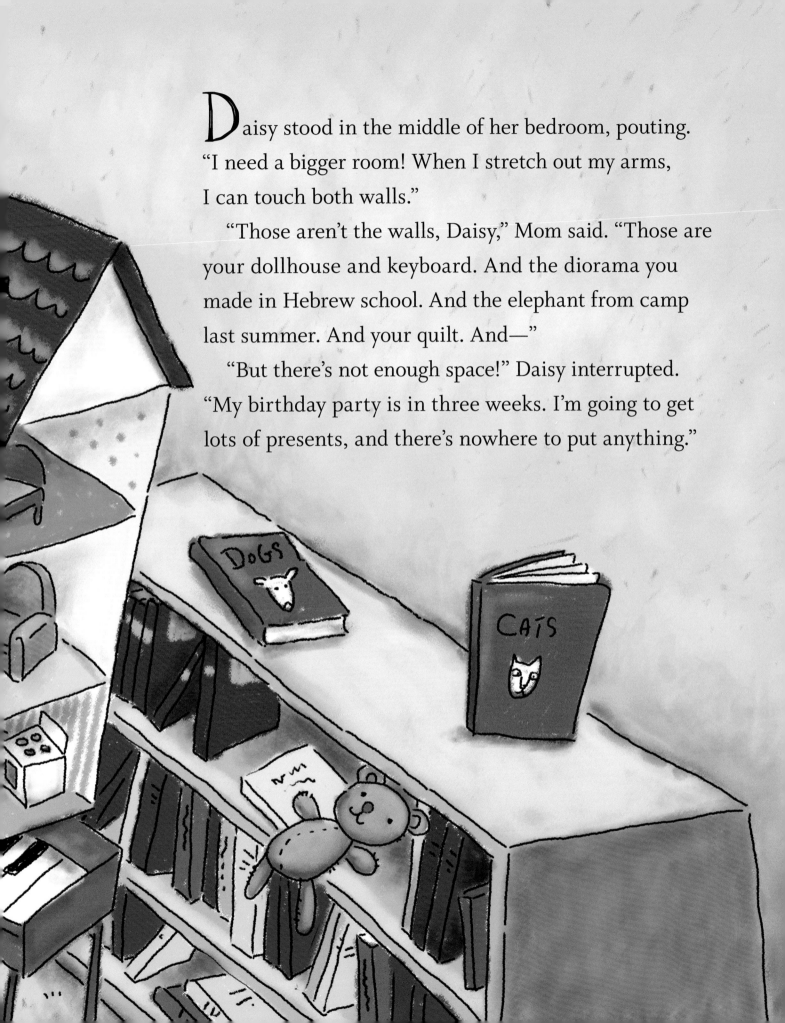

Daisy stood in the middle of her bedroom, pouting. "I need a bigger room! When I stretch out my arms, I can touch both walls."

"Those aren't the walls, Daisy," Mom said. "Those are your dollhouse and keyboard. And the diorama you made in Hebrew school. And the elephant from camp last summer. And your quilt. And—"

"But there's not enough space!" Daisy interrupted. "My birthday party is in three weeks. I'm going to get lots of presents, and there's nowhere to put anything."

"How do you know you're getting lots of presents?" Mom asked.

"Look what's on my list!"

"A hockey net? You have a perfectly good hockey net in the backyard."

"I need one to practice *inside*," Daisy said. "Besides, the old one has a hole in it."

"And an aquarium?" Mom sounded confused.

"For fish."

"You don't have fish," Mom said.

"You haven't finished reading my list," Daisy pointed out.

"It's awfully long," Mom said as she picked up Daisy's quilt from the floor. "Do you really think you need a bigger room?"

"Yes!"

Mom handed Daisy the quilt. "I have an idea," she said. "I'll be right back."

Daisy dumped the quilt on her bed and flopped on top. Life was so unfair. Her best friend, Amanda, had a huge bedroom with a closet bigger than Daisy's entire room. Daisy's parents had the biggest room in the house. She was trying to figure out how to convince them to trade rooms when her mother appeared in the doorway. Her face was hidden behind an enormous box.

"This is a special box," Mom said.

"What's so special about it?" Daisy asked.

Mom opened the box with a flourish. "This box will make your room bigger."

"This is all my old stuff!" Daisy said. "It's supposed to be in the basement."

"It was supposed to go to the synagogue for last year's Mitzvah Day rummage sale," Mom reminded her.

Daisy frowned. "But then you said we could wait to decide. And I've decided. It's my stuff. I want to keep it."

"Okay," Mom said. "You can keep it. Right here."

"In my room?"

"That's what your room's for," Mom said.

"But there's no space. My room's too small."

"Let's unpack the box together."

Before Daisy could say another word,
Mom began pulling out stuff Daisy hadn't
thought about in years.

"I had three tea sets?" Daisy asked.

"You liked to entertain," Mom said.

Daisy reached into the box. "I remember this."
She held up a large plastic purse. "It's the goody
bag from Stephanie's birthday party."

Mom opened it. "Ooof. This stinks."
She tossed the purse into the garbage.

Daisy fished it out. "I want to keep it.
It was an awesome party. Missy threw up
all over Stephanie's new couch."

"Is that why the purse stinks?" Mom asked.

Daisy didn't answer. She'd found a little bear dressed in a suit with a plaid bow tie. "What's this?"

"That's Maxie. You slept with Maxie every night when you were a baby."

"How come I stopped?" Daisy asked.

Mom shrugged. "People gave you lots of other stuff."

Daisy waited all week for the contents of the box to
make her room bigger. Each morning she climbed out of
bed and stretched out her arms. But the walls seemed to
be moving closer instead of farther away. And whenever
she tripped over the plastic purse—this happened a lot—
she twisted herself up in the dress-up clothes and crashed
onto the tea sets. By the end of the week, she was covered
with bruises the size of golf balls.

"Mom!" she hollered on Saturday morning as she lay
in the middle of the floor, rubbing the lump on her shin.
"This isn't working. My room isn't getting bigger.
It's shrinking. And my party is only two weeks away."

Mom appeared in the doorway. She was pulling something behind her. "This should fix it. Close your eyes."

Daisy put her hands over her face.

"No peeking," Mom said.

Daisy heard something being dragged across the carpet. A horrible smell, like sweaty socks soaked in a toilet bowl, drifted toward her. Daisy squeezed her eyes shut and pinched her nose.

"Okay. Open your eyes."

"My goalie pads? My hockey net?"

"You said you wanted to practice inside. Now you can."

"But, Mom, this isn't fixing anything. It's making it worse!"

"Trust me," Mom said. "It's helping."

Another week went by. Daisy waited for the goalie pads and the hockey net to make her room bigger. Each morning she climbed out of bed and stretched out her arms. But the walls still seemed to be moving closer. And whenever she stumbled over the goalie pads—this happened a lot—she tumbled into the net, tripped over the plastic purse, twisted herself up in the dress-up clothes and crashed onto the tea sets. By the end of the week, she was covered with bruises the size of hockey pucks.

"Mom!" she hollered on Saturday morning as she lay in the middle of the floor, rubbing the bump on her elbow. "This isn't working. My room isn't getting bigger. It's shrinking. And my party is next week!"

Mom appeared in the doorway. "I have
a solution." She dragged a black metal table
into the only clear spot in the room.

Just looking at it made Daisy's bumps
and bruises hurt. "What's that?" she asked.

"It's a stand for the aquarium on your
birthday list," Mom said.

"Oh," Daisy said in a small voice. "Mom, how is an aquarium stand supposed to help?"

"Trust me," Mom said.

During the next week, Daisy waited for the aquarium stand to make her room bigger. Each morning she climbed out of bed and stretched out her arms. But the walls absolutely seemed to be moving closer. And whenever she bumped into the stand—this happened a lot—she stumbled over her goalie pads, tumbled into the net, tripped over the plastic purse, twisted herself up in the dress-up clothes and crashed onto the tea sets. By the end of the week, she was covered with bruises the size of soccer balls.

On the morning of her birthday party, Daisy lay in the middle of the floor, rubbing the bruise on her forehead as she stared at all her stuff. Even Amanda didn't have this much. Daisy looked around for Maxie. She had lost him again.

"Mom," she called out.

Mom appeared in the doorway.

"Where's that special box?" Daisy asked. "I have some things for the next rummage sale."

"What a splendid idea," Mom said.

Into the special box went the stuffed animals, tea sets, dolls, dollhouse, elephant and keyboard.

"I should throw this away," Daisy said, holding up the smelly plastic purse. "And the diorama."

"What about Maxie?" Mom asked.

Daisy hugged the bear, which had turned up between a teapot and a box of dried-out markers. "I'm keeping him," she said. "But can we give the aquarium stand away? I think I really only want a goldfish bowl."

"What if you get an aquarium for your birthday?"

Daisy sighed. Her party was only four hours away. It was too late to call everyone and tell them she didn't want any gifts. "Do you think there's room in the box for some of my presents?"

Mom smiled. "It *is* a special box," she said.

Daisy had the best birthday party ever. And that night, when she stood in the middle of her room and stretched out her arms, she couldn't even reach her desk or her bookshelves.

She lifted Maxie off the bed and twirled around the room, cuddling him close. "Look at this," she said to him. "I have the perfect room."

What's Mitzvah Day?

Mitzvah means "commandment" in Hebrew, although the word has also come to mean "good deed." Included in the 613 commandments handed to Moses on Mount Sinai are instructions to give back to the community, take care of the environment and practice *tzedakah* (charity).

Mitzvah Day is a way to do these things. Some communities host multiple Mitzvah Day events throughout the year. These can include staffing soup kitchens, cleaning up local parks and cemeteries, helping at seniors' homes and making quilts or knitting clothing for those in need. Other typical activities are collecting items to send to victims of war or natural disasters, restocking local food banks, hosting blood drives and raising money for charities. Daisy's synagogue holds an annual rummage sale, which helps the larger community and the environment too.